and the
Flea Circus

anthony ant

and the
Flea Circus

STORY BY JOHN GRANT

Based on the TV series

INSPIRED BY THE BOOKS OF LORNA AND GRAHAM PHILPOT

A Dolphin ★ Paperback

First published in Great Britain in 1999
as a Dolphin Paperback
by Orion Children's Books
a division of the Orion Publishing Group Ltd
Orion House
5 Upper St Martin's Lane
London WC2H 9EA

TV series copyright © HIT Entertainment Plc and YTV co-productions 1999
Based on the books by Lorna and Graham Philpot
Illustrations by The County Studio
Illustrations copyright © Orion Children's Books 1999

The right of John Grant to be identified as the author of this work
has been asserted.

A catalogue record for this book is available from the British Library.
Printed in Great Britain

Antville was buzzing with excitement. The circus was coming! And it wasn't just any old circus. It was Lord Fancy-Flea and his Fabulous Flea Circus.

Anthony was standing in front of the museum in the town square with his mother and Grandpa Angus. They were looking at the poster that had just been put up. Anthony was full of questions. He had never seen a flea circus, but the older ants could remember the last time

"CIRCUS!"

MIGHTY POWER FLEA

LOVE BEAUTY-FLEA

Lord Fancy-Flea had come to Antville. Grandpa Angus had a faraway look as he recalled it.

"Och aye," he said, "I'll never forget the Lovely Beauty-Flea. High on the tightrope, light as air. And the Flying Grace-Fleas on the trapeze! Those were the days!"

"I was just a silly young ant then," said Anthony's mother dreamily. "I remember losing my heart to the Mighty Power-Flea.

He made the biggest ant look like a weakling."

"What did he do?" asked Anthony.

"What did he do? He pulled a four-aphid coach round and round the circus ring all by himself."

"Look, he's starring this time too!" said Anthony, studying the poster. "And so are the Lovely Beauty-Flea and the Flying Grace-Fleas. They must all be very, very old indeed!"

"Och, no," laughed Grandpa. "Those aren't their real names. Their fathers and mothers and grannies and grandpas were called the Mighty Power-Flea and the Lovely Beauty Flea and the Flying Grace-Fleas too."

"Oh," said Anthony. "I hadn't thought of that."

Everyone watched the big parade as the

circus rolled into town. Anthony, Alexi, Kevin, Terry, Ruby and Billy wanted to see everything.

Leading the parade was a brightly painted wagon drawn by a pair of sturdy aphids, and carrying the circus band who were playing a lively march tune. Just behind came Lord Fancy-Flea himself, riding a prancing black aphid. He waved grandly to the crowds.

Wagon after wagon passed by, carrying the circus performers. There was the

Mighty Power-Flea, flexing his muscles. Then there was the Lovely Beauty-Flea, not on a tightrope but twirling a parasol and blowing kisses to the crowds. And near the end of the parade came a cage of roaring ant-lions with their tamer, the brave Captain Man-Flea, cracking his whip.

Anthony and the gang clapped and cheered. Billy jumped for joy when he saw the clowns. He wished he could be a clown. Perhaps a sad-faced one like Dole-Flea, or a jolly one like the smiling Cheer-Flea.

The parade went through the town to a big field outside, and the circus hands started putting up the Big Top while Lord Fancy-Flea rode to the palace. He wanted to invite the Queen and Princess Antoinette to be guests of honour at the opening performance. They were delighted to accept.

It was a pity that Count Mosquito was out of the palace at the time, and that Lord Fancy-Flea didn't invite him to be a guest of honour too. Because when Count Mosquito heard about it he was furious!

Count Mosquito was a very important person. He was probably the most important person at the palace. The Queen always took his advice. The palace staff were scared of him. So it was a terrible insult when he wasn't asked to the circus. And Count Mosquito wasn't going to let Lord Fancy-Flea get away with it.

While Antville slept, the Count plotted. He couldn't stop the Queen and Princess Antoinette going to the circus, but perhaps he could stop the circus playing . . .

The Count sent for his two gnat nephews, Buzz and Nate.

"I have a mission for you," he said. "It is of the utmost importance. I may say –" he paused "– even, very grave."

"Hey, boss," said Buzz. "Did you say

'grave'? Not the old graveyard?"

"It's spooky!" said Nate. "It's creepy! Anywhere but . . ."

"Fools!" shouted the Count. "I'm not talking about graves. It's circus performers. They have to be removed . . . temporarily. No performers, no circus. No circus, no guests of honour. Get it?"

"But I think . . ." said Nate.

"But I don't think . . ." said Buzz.

"Don't even think about thinking, you pair of flea-brains!" shrieked the Count. "Now, pay attention. This is what you do." And he told Buzz and Nate which of the performers were to be lured away and kept out of sight.

Before he had finished, Buzz and Nate were both talking at once.

"Boss, you can't mean it!"

"Get someone else to do it!"

"We'll get it all wrong! Please . . . !"

"Not the Mighty Power-Flea! He bends iron bars with his bare hands. He'll tear us apart!"

"Be cunning," snarled the Count. "Brain over brawn. Brain? Mmm, that's going to be a problem. You're going to have to find a place to hide them."

"Can't we just ask them round here?" said Buzz.

"For a cup of tea?" said Nate.

"Not here!" snapped the Count. "Keep me out of it. Just go and find somewhere. And don't be all day about it. You've only got until three this afternoon!"

Meanwhile, Anthony and the gang were watching the performers getting ready for the show. Some were rehearsing their acts. Kevin watched a pair of jugglers, juggling with balls, hoops and knives.

"That's cool," said Kevin. He desperately wanted to be a good juggler.

Then they started juggling with flaming torches.

"Wow!" Kevin marvelled, "that's amazing."

Billy Bedbug went in search of the clowns. He spotted two of them in a large tent. He slipped inside and hid behind a wicker basket. The clowns were putting on

their make-up, and didn't notice him. One looked very unhappy.

"That must be Dole-Flea," thought Billy.

But the sad clown painted on a broadly smiling mouth. And the clown with the happy grin gave himself a painted face that was so sad Billy almost felt like crying. What a muddling place the circus was!

Billy was about to follow the clowns out of the tent when he heard voices. Voices he knew. Buzz and Nate. Not good company for a young bedbug. He must hide.

He lifted the lid of the wicker basket and saw that it was filled with costumes. As he slipped into the basket and pulled the lid shut he saw Buzz and Nate duck inside the tent. They must be up to something.

"O.K., so we find Power-Flea. And we say a very good friend wants you away from here until after three o'clock."

It was Nate's voice.

"Dimbo!" That was Buzz. "We've got to be what the boss said — cunning. Tell him a story so he wants to come with us."

"Like his grandma's just died?" said Nate.

"How do we know he's got a grandma?" said Buzz. "I don't have a grandma."

"But it isn't you the boss wants out of the way until three o'clock." said Nate. "And anyway, I just remembered something. There's a Bigfoot sort of thing among the rose bushes near the pond. Leave it to me."

Billy heard Buzz and Nate leave the tent. This was an emergency. When Buzz and Nate were up to something, Count Mosquito wasn't far away. And when the Count wasn't far away, it meant trouble for someone. This time it was the Mighty Power-Flea. He had to find Anthony.

Anthony and the gang were watching Captain Man-Flea and his ferocious ant-lions. The Captain cracked his whip and the ant-lions leapt up on to painted tubs. The biggest ant-lion roared and snarled. But Captain Man-flea never flinched. He cracked his whip again and the ant-lion leaped through a flaming hoop.

"That's cruel," said Ruby. "Those poor

creatures should be out roaming the wild, not doing silly tricks in a circus." She was going to say more, but at that moment Billy ran up, panting.

"Quick! It's an emergency! No time to lose! We've got to stop them!"

"What emergency? Stop who?" asked Anthony.

"Keep cool, Billy," said Kevin. "Take a deep breath. Give us facts. Name names!"

"Buzz and Nate," said Billy.

"It's an emergency. It figures," said Kevin.

Billy went on. "It's the Mighty Power-Flea. They're going to keep him away from the circus until after three o'clock."

"Circus wreckers!" cried Anthony. "If the Mighty Power-Flea isn't there, the show will be ruined!"

And, even as he spoke, there was a shout from the Big Top. Lord Fancy-Flea stormed out.

"Disaster!" he cried. "The Intrepid Captain Wonder-Flea is in bed with measles. And now the Mighty Power-Flea, the Lovely Beauty-Flea and all the Flying

Grace-Fleas have vanished! I'm ruined. It will be the end of Lord Fancy-Flea's Fabulous Flea Circus!"

"So it's not just the Mighty Power-Flea," said Anthony. "Buzz and Nate must have got them all. Somebody doesn't want the show to go on. I wonder if Count Mosquito's got anything to do with this." He ran over to Lord Fancy-Flea.

"We think the Mighty Power-Flea, the Lovely Beauty-Flea and the Flying Grace-Fleas have been abducted!"

"Flea-napped," said Kevin.

"But who would do such a thing?" cried Lord Fancy-Flea.

"Billy heard two villains planning the whole thing," said Anthony. "We'll find them. Leave it to us. We have several hours yet."

"And if you don't find them in time?"

"We will take their places," said Anthony. "Perhaps not exactly. But we will do our best. The show must go on. The show will go on!"

"Now, Billy," said Alexi. "Tell us. Where have Buzz and Nate taken the Mighty

Power-Flea, the Lovely Beauty-Flea and all the Flying Grace-Fleas?"

"I don't know," said Billy. "Nate said something about a place he knows. A sort of Bigfoot thing, he called it. Near the pond. Among the roses."

"It's a start," said Ruby. "But what on earth can there be in a rosebed to hide one strong flea, one tightrope-walking flea and four trapeze-swinging fleas?"

"A Bigfoot flowerpot," suggested Alexi.

"Nope!" said Kevin. "Fleas jump. Wow! How they can jump. There's no way you're going to keep a flea in a flowerpot."

"Bigfoot matchbox," suggested Terry.

"How do you persuade six performing fleas to jump into a matchbox?" said Anthony.

"Good point," said Kevin. "Why don't we head for the pond and the roses? You never know what we might find."

"Let's go, gang," said Anthony.

Keeping a wary eye on Count Mosquito's castle, the gang skirted the pond.

Ahead lay the deep shadows and prickly thorns of the rosebed. It was dark and damp under the rose bushes. Slugs left slimy trails

across the bare earth. Overhead, greenfly clung to leaves and stems, watching the

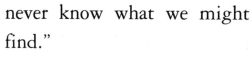

gang as they picked their way warily
between mouldy leaves.

three

"**W**hat are we looking for?" asked Alexi, in a hushed voice.

"That's a good question," said Kevin. "Hey! What's that?" Between the thorny twigs he had caught a glimpse of a strange square object on the ground.

"I think it's some kind of Bigfoot thing," said Billy. "Nate spoke of something like that."

"It's got Bigfoot written all over it," said Kevin. "Listen! Do you hear something?"

"Noises!" said Ruby. "Insect noises. Very angry insect noises. It's a prison."

"It's a Bigfoot bug trap," said Alexi. "I knew a ladybird who was caught in one once. She was lucky to escape."

"This must be the place," said Anthony.

He put his hands to his mouth and shouted as loudly as he could.

"Hello in there! Are there any fleas among you?"

"Too right there are!" came back an

angry voice from inside the bug trap. "Just let me get my hands on those two nasty gnats!"

"That," said Kevin, "in my opinion, is one very irate flea. The Mighty Power-Flea, no doubt. I almost feel sorry for Buzz and Nate."

"Is there a way in?" called Anthony.

"It's out we want!" The Mighty Power-Flea was getting impatient. "There's a sort of circular door thing. It doesn't open from this side. It's on a kind of pivot thing. It's pretty big."

"Meant for Bigfoot fingers," said Terry. "Let's have a look." He scrambled up over some fallen twigs and on to the trap itself. "It's round the other side. Yes, it's a sort of pivot. Shouldn't be much of a problem."

The rest of the gang hurried round in time to see Terry clinging to the pivot disc.

He swung it one way and then the other. "It's coming loose!" he panted. "Everyone look out below!"

There was a loud crack. The gang jumped back as a large wooden disc crashed to the ground. Terry hung by his fingers from a round opening. He scrambled to the top of the bug trap.

"Everybody out!" he called. And a crowd of fleas sprang out in a hurry.

"What happened?" asked Anthony.

"We were fooled," sobbed the Lovely Beauty-Flea.

"Those wretched gnats said they were fans," growled the Mighty Power-Flea.

"They told us," said the Flying Grace-Fleas, speaking all together, "that our fan club was waiting to welcome us in the clubroom. That box thing."

"You can still make it back in time for the show," said Anthony. "Do you know the way?"

"Yes," said the Mighty Power-Flea. "Come, ladies and gentlemen. Our public awaits us." And, in one enormous leap, they were out of sight.

"Look at them go!" cried Kevin.

"They'll be at the circus before we get

as far as the pond," said Anthony. "We'd better hurry!"

Close to the edge of the rosebed they heard voices. As they crouched behind a stout rose stem, the owners of the voices came into sight.

"You got the time?" said Buzz.

"Yup!" replied Nate. "And we don't let those fleas out until after three o' clock."

"You do know how to open it to let them out?" asked Buzz.

"I thought you knew. You told me you were an expert."

"Oh, I'll figure it out. All in good time . . ."

"Hello, boys," said Anthony. "We've just been having a chat with some of the circus folk. The big, strong one. And the pretty lady flea. And the ones that perform on the trapeze. Nice insects. Hurrying off to get ready. We'd better hurry too. Wouldn't want to miss Lord Fancy-Flea's Fabulous Flea Circus. Bye now!"

Buzz and Nate stood open-mouthed as the gang went on their way.

"I think they got out," said Nate.

"I think they were let out," said Buzz.

"What'll the boss say?" said Nate in a panic-stricken voice.

"Don't even think about it," said Buzz. Meanwhile, everyone at the circus was hurrying and bustling. As the gang arrived, Lord Fancy-Flea ran up to them. "You did it!" he cried. "My stars are back! What can I do to reward you?"

"Remember we offered to perform in the circus if the stars couldn't be found in time?" said Anthony. "Well, we'd still like to do it."

"Not me," said Alexi. "Not in front of an audience. Can I be the girl who comes out at the interval and sells snacks?"

"Of course! Of course!" cried Lord Fancy-Flea. "Come, all of you, and we'll see what we can do to turn you into circus people."

Back in his own castle, Count Mosquito waited. The clock struck three. The Count smiled an evil smile. Then he frowned. What was that he could hear? Music? He opened a window. Faintly but clearly came the sound of a stirring tune, 'March of the Mayflies'. Played by a band! The circus! The show was about to begin!

The Count jumped up and down, waved

his arms and screamed, "Flea-brained fools! I should have known better! Wait till I get my hands on them! I'll . . .! I'll . . .!"

He paused. "Perhaps it's all bluff. Old Fancy-Flea is keeping the band playing to keep the audience amused while he waits for his stars to arrive. No stars! No circus! There will be a riot! This I must see!"

And he set off as fast as he could for the circus.

As the Count drew near the circus the music stopped. There was laughter coming from the Big Top, then applause, then more laughter. He sneaked round the back for a closer look. A voice said, "Can I help you? I'm afraid there are no seats left for this performance. It's a sell-out."

It was Lord Fancy-Flea.

"Ah, jolly good! Well done!" said the Count. He was thinking, "So, those two idiots did get it wrong. I'll enjoy dealing with them when . . ."

But Lord Fancy-Flea was speaking again. "We nearly had to cancel, but some nice young ants came to the rescue."

"Had I known," smiled the Count, "I'm sure I could have been of some help."

"Perhaps you still can be," said Lord Fancy-Flea. "One of my stars is sick. The Intrepid Captain Wonder-Flea. His act usually closes the show. If only I . . ."

"My dear fellow," exclaimed the Count. "Your troubles are over. I myself am not without experience in show business. I shall be your intrepid Captain."

"But do you think you can . . . ?"

"Please," interrupted the Count. "I have skills too numerous to mention."

"In that case," said Lord Fancy-Flea

with relief, "be at the costume wagon in an hour. Now I must go to announce the next act. And thank you."

"My pleasure," said the Count as Lord Fancy-Flea disappeared into the Big Top, "my performance will be the talk of Antville and beyond."

four

While the Count was offering to be Captain Wonder-Flea, a circus hand came up to the gang. "So you want to join the circus, do you?" he said.

"Just for today," said Anthony.

"Right, come to the costume wagon. Tell Madame Fancy-Flea what your act is. She'll fit you up with an outfit to suit." He led them to a large wagon. An elderly flea looked at them over her spectacles.

"We'll start with you, young ant," she

said to Kevin.

"Well – er – I'm a juggler, sort of. You know. Balls and things," Kevin stammered, suddenly feeling very uncool.

Madame Fancy-Flea ran a measuring tape over Kevin. She made some notes.

"Next!" she said. It was Billy.

"Please, I'd like to be a clown," said Billy. "With a smiling face and baggy trousers. And a big red nose." Madame Fancy-Flea measured him too.

Anthony said he was going to do tricks on a skateboard. Madame Fancy-Flea looked and said, "Medium. Normal." Then she nodded to Terry. "You're the strong one, aren't you? We've got a special place for you in the show." And she wrote 'Large, very' in her notebook.

Now it was Ruby's turn. "When I was little my Grandpa taught me some things," she said. "How about it if I do some rope-spinning?"

"She sings, too," said Anthony.

"A singing rope-spinner," said Madame Fancy-Flea. "I've got just the thing for you. Used to belong to Hop-Along Hope-Flea, Smartest Flea in the West. And for our young snackseller, I have a very smart uniform." She smiled at Alexi.

Things began to move quickly. The circus hand hustled the gang to a tent behind the Big Top, where they could hear the music blaring out. Madame Fancy-Flea brought in the costumes – a matching cap and jacket with sequins on for Anthony, a

baggy clown suit for Billy and a spangled overcoat for Terry. Kevin was surprised to get a clown suit too.

But it was Ruby's costume that made them all gasp. A high-crowned, broad-brimmed white hat, a fringed white jacket and skirt, and a pair of white, knee-high cowboy boots. "If only my grandpa could see me," she said.

The clowns, Dole-Flea and Cheer-Flea, came in. "Right, Billy," said Dole-Flea cheerfully, "we're on in a moment. Don't worry. We'll tell you what to do."

"I don't like having beginners in the act," grumbled Cheer-Flea. "Just don't get in the way."

From the Big Top they heard Lord Fancy-Flea.

"And now, ladies and gentlemen, your old favourites . . . Dole-Flea and Cheer-Flea!

And . . . a guest appearance by that young star . . . Bouncing Billy Bedbug!"

Everyone clapped as the two clowns ran into the ring with Billy behind them. The

clowns bounced on a trampoline, turned somersaults and tumbled over and over, tossing Billy about till he didn't know if he was on his head or his heels. The audience roared, and Billy took a bow with the clowns, beaming.

Kevin's turn came next. The circus hand gave him a set of juggling balls as he went on. He stood in the spotlight, gulped, and started to juggle. But something wasn't right. He had been given trick balls! They had a life of their own. They wobbled in the air and bounced in all sorts of unexpected directions. But Kevin kept going. He juggled as he had never juggled before. And the crowd loved it. Suddenly the balls all shot off in different directions. Kevin gave up. He stood in the centre of the ring, almost in tears.

Lord Fancy-Flea came into the ring. "A big hand, now, ladies and gentlemen, for Kevin the Comedy Juggler. A real master of his art!"

And Kevin went off with cheers and laughter ringing in his ears.

"They really liked me!" he said. "That's cool! Really cool!"

Anthony's skateboarding was not quite what he had expected. He had never done it to music before! And it wasn't his kind of music either! The band started with a brisk march, then a slow waltz. He did a super two-wheel reverse pirouette to a lively jig, and finished the act with a dazzling show of slow wheelies to a cha-cha-cha.

Then there was a short interval. It was Alexi's turn to move through the audience selling cartons of cool honeydew and crunchy poppy seed bars. A familiar voice called, "I'd like a carton of honeydew, please." It was Princess Antoinette, in the Royal Box. "I didn't know my friends were circus people," she said.

"It's only for today," said Alexi.

"I wish I could take part," sighed Antoinette.

At that moment, Lord Fancy-Flea entered the ring. The audience hushed.

"Ladies and gentlemen, I am proud to present for your enjoyment an act that will truly amaze you."

The band struck up, 'Get Along Little Aphid'. And there in the spotlight stood Ruby. She carried a lasso in each hand. She flicked one out into a wide loop and spun it, faster and faster. The loop grew wider and wider, until she stood in the centre of the whirling rope. The audience cheered, but there was more. A second rope spun out. And another. And another. Ruby was spinning four ropes at the same time!

She looked up to the band and nodded. As she spun her ropes, the band played and she sang:

"She'll be comin' round the anthill when she comes . . .!"

The audience stamped, clapped and joined in. They had never seen anything like it before.

Ruby left the ring. The applause died down. It was almost time for the Intrepid Captain Wonder-Flea.

Count Mosquito was not happy in the Intrepid Captain Wonder-Flea's costume. It was not a good fit. Fleas on the whole are tubby. Mosquitoes, on the other hand, are very slim, and have wings. The tunic was uncomfortably tight and the trousers were far too baggy.

The Count looked at himself in a long mirror. "I don't look my best," he thought, "but whatever it is I have to do as Captain Wonder-Flea, I will do it with style, even elegance." He looked around the dressing tent for some clue to what the Captain did in his act, but could see nothing. He would know soon enough.

Lord Fancy-Flea looked in. "Ready for you in a few minutes," he said. "And . . . eh . . . break a leg!"

"What? What?" cried the Count. "Oh! Of course! That means good luck. I had clean forgotten!"

A moment later, he heard Lord Fancy-Flea's voice from inside the ring.

"Ladies and gentlemen! This is what you have been waiting for – the climax to Lord Fancy-Flea's Fabulous Flea Circus! A big hand now for the brave, the courageous, the Intrepid Captain Wonder-Flea!"

"That's you. You're on," said a circus hand. And, with what he hoped was a brave and courageous expression on his face, the Count strode into the ring and bowed to the audience.

He was aware of an odd creaking and rumbling coming from behind him. He turned. And his heart sank. A section of the Big Top had been moved aside and an enormous cannon was coming into the ring, pulled by a team of fleas led by Terry Termite.

The Count gulped. There was something happening overhead. A section of the canvas was being rolled back to show the sky.

"Captain Wonder-Flea will now prepare to be shot from the cannon," announced Lord Fancy-Flea.

"Not if I can help it!" cried the Count. "You didn't tell me!"

"You didn't ask," said Lord Fancy-Flea. "And you can't let your public down."

"They're not my public. I don't know them. We haven't been introduced."

"I just introduced you," said Lord Fancy-Flea. "Didn't you hear? Now, up you go. There's a good chap."

The Count was pushed up a ladder, struggling, and into the barrel of the cannon.

"That's right," said Lord Fancy-Flea. "Make it look as if you don't want to go. The audience will think it's dangerous."

"But it is dangerous!" shrieked the Count, kicking and screaming.

"It's quite all right, there's a safety net," said Lord Fancy-Flea.

The Count tried to climb out again.

But at that moment the barrel was tilted up to aim at the opening in the roof and he slid right down inside.

"All ready?" asked Lord Fancy-Flea.

"He's a lot lighter than the other Captain Wonder-Flea," said the circus hand in charge of the cannon. "We should have moved the safety net farther away."

"Too late now," said Lord Fancy-Flea. He gave a signal to the band. There was a long drum roll, and he announced in a dramatic voice, "TEN SECONDS . . . and counting!"

And the audience joined in the count-down: "TEN . . . NINE . . . EIGHT . . . SEVEN . . . SIX . . . FIVE . . . FOUR . . . THREE . . . TWO . . . ONE . . . FIRE!!!!!"

There was a loud bang and a swoosh! The Count shot out of the cannon and through the opening in the roof of the Big Top!

Buzz and Nate heard the bang as they skulked in the grass at the edge of the pond.

"What was that?" yelped Nate.

"There's something falling out of the sky!" shrieked Buzz.

A strange object was hurtling down towards them.

"It's . . . it's . . ." gasped Nate.

"It can't be!" gulped Buzz.

But it was. With a horrible yell, the object collided head on with Buzz, who slammed into Nate.

With one enormous splash, Buzz, Nate and the strange object tumbled head over heels into the water.

Buzz and Nate were first out. They stood on the bank, dripping water, and watched the strange object as it crawled up the bank.

"Aaaarrrgh!" screamed Count Mosquito, lunging at his nephews.

But Buzz and Nate had flown away in a hurry. They didn't want to be anywhere near the Count when he found out what had happened.

Back at the circus there was panic. Where was Captain Wonder-Flea? He hadn't landed in the safety net. The whole company and most of the audience ran out to look for him.

"What a shame he wasn't heavier," said Lord Fancy-Flea. "He must have landed miles away."

Before long the search party gave up and turned back, but Anthony and the gang pressed on. And, there by the pond, they found a very wet and bedraggled Count Mosquito. Captain Wonder-Flea's costume lay in a soggy heap.

"Wow!" cried Anthony, "that was quite a stunt. Perhaps you should think about joining the circus permanently."

But the Count merely said, "Bah!" and retired to his castle.

Anthony said, "Well, gang, it was fun being a circus performer. But I don't think I'd want to do it often."

The others agreed.

Except Billy. "One day," he said to himself, "I shall run off and join the circus for real."